WESTMINSTER SCHOOLS

SMYTHE GAMBRELL
LIBRARY

PRESENTED BY

Marshall
Binford

Cate Candler

EMMA
by James Stevenson

GREENWILLOW BOOKS

NEW YORK

Library of Congress Cataloging in Publication Data
Stevenson, James, (date) Emma.
Summary: With the help of her friends, and after a few false
starts, a young witch named Emma learns to fly on her broom.
[1. Witches—Fiction.   2. Flight—Fiction] I. Title.
PZ7.S84748Em 1985 [E] 84-4141
ISBN 0-688-04020-9   ISBN 0-688-04021-7 (lib. bdg.)

THE BROOM WENT UP INTO THE TREE, LAVINIA...
...ALL BY ITSELF, DOLORES!

SWEET DREAMS, BROOM!
NOW EMMA'S TALKING TO THE BROOM?